For anyone who still sleeps with the lights on

IMPRINT
A part of Macmillan Publishing Group, LLC
175 Fifth Avenue, New York, NY 10010

ABOUT THIS BOOK
The art for this book is digital painting. The text was set in Burbank Small, and the display type was handlettered.
The book was edited by Rhoda Belleza and John Morgan and designed by Ellen Duda.
The production was supervised by Raymond Ernesto Colón, and the production editor was Dawn Ryan.

It's Not a Bed It's a Time Machine. Text copyright © 2019 by Navy Court, Inc.
Illustrations copyright © 2019 by Imprint.
All rights reserved. Printed in China by Toppan Leefung Printing Ltd., Dongguan City, Guangdong Province.

Library of Congress Cataloging-in-Publication Data is available.
ISBN 978-1-250-16762-0 (hardcover)

Our books may be purchased in bulk for promotional, educational, or business use. Please
contact your local bookseller or the Macmillan Corporate and Premium Sales Department at
(800) 221-7945 ext. 5442 or by email at MacmillanSpecialMarkets@macmillan.com.

Imprint logo designed by Amanda Spielman

First edition, 2019

1 3 5 7 9 10 8 6 4 2

mackids.com

"To sleep, perchance to dream?"
That's some Shakespeare spit.
Steal this book,
and be cursed with nightmares quick!

IT'S NOT A BED, IT'S A TIME MACHINE

Written by Mickey Rapkin

Illustrated by Teresa Martinez

[Imprint]
MAKE YOUR MARK

New York

"Good night, kiddo. Be brave.
You're the Boss of Bedtime!"

Me? Brave?
I wasn't so sure.

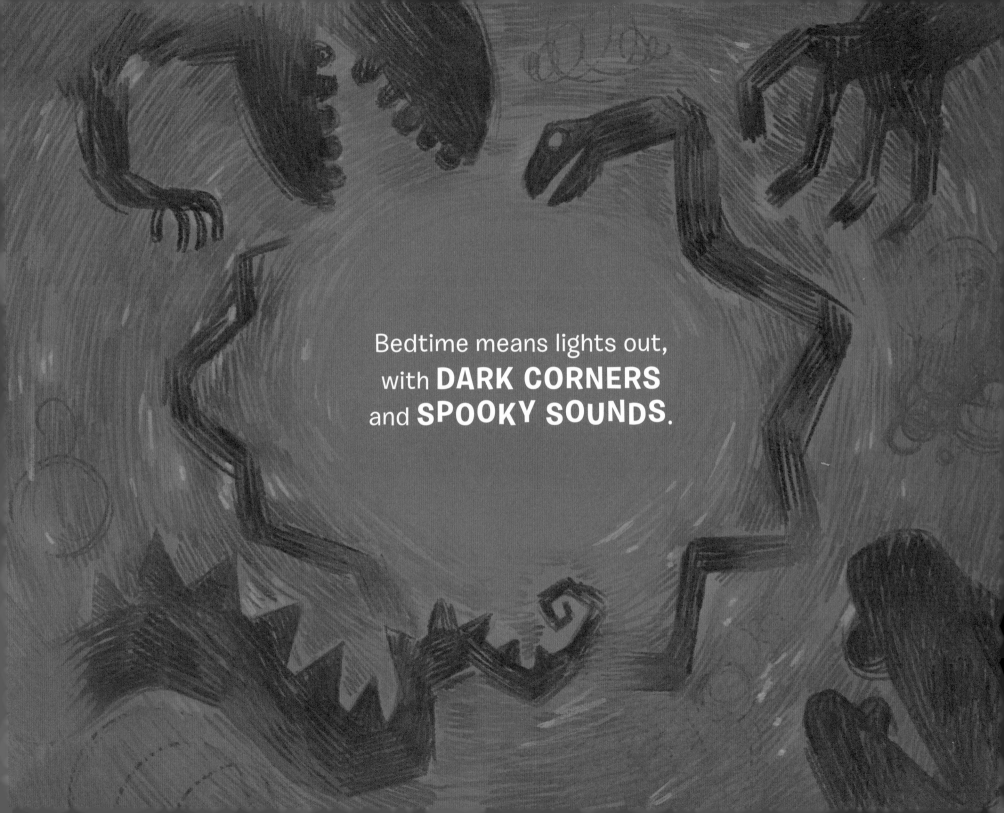

Bedtime means lights out,
with **DARK CORNERS**
and **SPOOKY SOUNDS**.

"Don't be afraid of bedtime," Floppy said.
"This isn't a bed . . . it's a

TIME MACHINE!

"Think about it!" Floppy said. "You brush your teeth, get under the covers, and then what? **BAM!** It's morning. Where did the hours go?"

"Close your eyes. Imagine your next adventure. Then it's blastoff in **5-4-3-2-FUN!"**

You know what I saw next?
I'll give you one tyrannosaurus guess . . .

DINOSAURS!

HUNDREDS OF 'EM!

"Whoa, whoa, wait a minute! Is this safe?" Floppy mumbled.

But I was already climbing
a tree branch . . . which
wasn't a tree branch at all.

It was a dinosaur!
Floppy shouted:

RUN!

Then the dinosaur . . . licked my hair?

SLURP!

"You're not scary," I said. "You just wanna play!"
So, we played fetch with his giant bone.

And we played Connect the Dots
with twinkly stars.

It would have been awesome to hang for six billion years, but I started missing home.

We tried to leave, but my new friend
wouldn't stop nibbling on my sock.
"I don't think he wants to
be alone," Floppy whispered.

"But you're not alone, Dino-pal," I said.
"The other dinosaurs are always nearby."

He had *his* family.
Now it was time for me to see mine.

Floppy and I climbed back into the time machine. "Be brave," Floppy whispered. "You're the Boss of Bedtime!"

When I opened my eyes again, the sun was peeking through.
"Look at your hair!" Mom said. "What happened?!"

"I had a dream my bed was
A TIME MACHINE!
**AND A DINOSAUR LICKED ME!
AND–AND–**"

Maybe it wasn't a dream after all . . .